Anonymous

AF138487

Acts and Resolutions of the Legislative Assembly of the Territory of Utah

Anatiposi

Anonymous

Acts and Resolutions of the Legislative Assembly of the Territory of Utah

Reprint of the original.

1st Edition 2023 | ISBN: 978-3-38230-076-0

Anatiposi Verlag is an imprint of Outlook Verlagsgesellschaft mbH.

Verlag (Publisher): Outlook Verlag GmbH, Zeilweg 44, 60439 Frankfurt, Deutschland
Vertretungsberechtigt (Authorized to represent): E. Roepke, Zeilweg 44, 60439 Frankfurt, Deutschland
Druck (Print): Books on Demand GmbH, In de Tarpen 42, 22848 Norderstedt, Deutschland

ACTS AND RESOLUTIONS

OF THE

LEGISLATIVE ASSEMBLY

OF THE

TERRITORY OF UTAH:

EIGHTH ANNUAL SESSION—FOR THE YEARS 1858-9.

ALSO

MEMORIALS TO CONGRESS.

GREAT SALT LAKE CITY, UTAH TERRITORY:
PRINTED BY J. McKNIGHT.

1859.

ACTS, RESOLUTIONS AND MEMORIALS

PASSED BY THE

UTAH LEGISLATIVE ASSEMBLY

AT THE

EIGHTH ANNUAL SESSION.

CHAP. I.—*Resolution to adjourn the Legislative Assembly of* Dec. 22, 1856, *Utah Territory, to Great Salt Lake City.*

Whereas, Fillmore City is inconveniently distant from the center of the present population of the Territory; the greater portion of the population residing in the northern counties, and

Whereas, the Offices and Residencies of the Governor and Territorial Secretary are in Great Salt Lake City, and no suitable accommodations can be procured in Fillmore City, either for them or the members of the Legislative Assembly, and

Whereas, for the foregoing reasons, the public interest will be best subserved by an adjournment to Great Salt Lake City, and

Whereas, by such an adjournment, the United States will not be subjected to any increased expense, as the Legislative Assembly hereby forego all claim to other than the ordinary and regular mileage, provided by law:—

Therefore, Be it resolved by the Governor and Legislative Assembly of the Territory of Utah, that the Legislative Assembly adjourn, to meet in the Social Hall, at Great Salt Lake City, on Monday, the twenty-seventh day of December, instant, at ten o'clock a.m.

APPROVED Dec. 22, 1858.

Jan. 21, 1859

Chap. II —*An Act prescribing certain Qualifications necessary to enable a Person to be eligible to hold office, vote or serve as a Juror.*

Sec. 1. *Be it enacted by the Governor and Legislative Assembly of the Territory of Utah,* that no person shall be elected a delegate to the Congress of the United States from this Territory who has not been a resident therein during one year next preceding the day of election.

Delegate one year's residence.

Sec. 2. No person shall be eligible to a seat in either branch of the Legislative Assembly unless he has been a resident in the county or district to be represented, during at least one year next preceding the day of election.

Legislator one year's residence.

Sec. 3. No person shall be elected or appointed to any territorial, district, county or precinct office unless he shall have been a constant resident therein during at least one year next preceding such election or appointment; neither shall any person be entitled to hold any office of trust or profit in the Territory or vote at any election unless he is a free, white male citizen of the United States, over twenty one years of age and has been a constant resident in the Territory during the six months next preceding said election or appointment.

All officers one year's residence.

Voters 6 months.

Sec. 4. A person is not eligible to serve and therefore shall not serve on any grand or petit jury in any court in this Territory unless he is a free, white male citizen of the United States, is over twenty one years of age, is of reputed sound mind and discretion, is not so disabled in body as to be unable to serve, has not been convicted of any capital or infamous crime, owns taxable property and pays taxes in this Territory, and has been a constant resident therein during the year last preceding his being selected to serve as a juror.

Jurors one year's residence.

Sec. 5. And be it further enacted, that no officer or soldier of the United States army or other person subject to their military authority is eligible to hold any office or serve on any jury or vote at any election in this Territory unless his home and place of residence was therein at the time of engaging in such service.

No officer or soldier of U. S. army can hold office or vote.

Sec. 6. No person shall be deemed a resident within the meaning of this act, unless he is a tax payer in this Territory.

Who are residents.

Sec. 7. All laws and parts of laws conflicting with this act are hereby repealed.

Approved Jan. 21, 1859.

Chap. III.—*An Act defining who are exempt from serving on Juries, and prescribing the mode of procuring Grand and Petit Jurors and Juries for District Courts, and for other purposes.* Jan. 21, 1859.

Sec. 1. *Be it enacted by the Governor and Legislative Assembly of the Territory of Utah,* that members and officers of the Legislative Assembly, Judges of Probate Courts, Select Men, County Treasurers, Clerks of the Persons exempt
Supreme, District, Probate and County Courts, the Territorial Marshal, Deputy Marshals, Sheriffs, Deputy Sheriffs, Constables, Attorneys and Counselors at law, persons at the time engaged in teaching school, Ferrymen, Millers, Physicians, Surgeons, and Editors of Newspapers and other periodical publications are exempt from serving either as grand or petit jurors.

Sec. 2. The County court in each county shall, at its first session in each year, and at such subsequent session or other time as a neglect so to do at said first List of Jurors, how made.
session or as other circumstances may require, make, from the assessment roll of the county, a list containing the names of at least fifty men, residents of the county, eligible to serve as jurors.

Sec. 3. Said list shall contain only the names of such persons as are known or believed to possess the requisite qualifications for jurors and not entitled to exemption from jury service; and the names thereon Names how apportioned.
shall be apportioned among the different sections of the county as nearly as may be, according to the names on the assessment roll; and the selections of persons to serve as jurors shall, from time to time, be made in such manner, so far as the County Court can judge, as to cause the eligible persons to perform jury duty as nearly as may be in rotation.

Sec. 4. Said list shall contain the christian and surname at length, and the place of residence and occupation of each person named therein, and shall be filed Filed with Clerk of County Court.
with the Clerk of the County Court, who shall keep in his office a box or other safe place of deposit, in which he shall deposit the names on the list, having previously written each name on a separate ticket and so folded said ticket that the name thereon does not appear.

Sec. 5. When a District Court is to be held, whether for a district or for a county, the Clerk of said court shall, at least thirty days previous to the time of holding said court, issue a writ to a Marshal or any of his deputies, if said court is to be holden for a district, or to the Sheriff or any of his deputies of the county in which said court is to be held, if it is to be held for a county, specifying the time and place of holding said court, and requiring him to summon, if for a grand jury, twenty four eligible men to serve as grand jurors, and, if for petit jurors, twenty four eligible men to serve as petit jurors; and said twenty four men shall constitute a grand jury; and said twenty four men shall constitute two full petit juries.

Thirty days previous to holding District Court issue writ for Jurors.

24 Grand—24 Petit Jurors.

Sec. 6. Upon the reception said writ, a Marshal or a Sheriff, as the case may be, or either of their deputies, shall proceed to the Clerk of the County Court of the county in which jurors are to be summoned, and said Clerk shall forthwith repair, with said officer having said writ, to the office of said Clerk, who shall, if a grand jury is required, in the presence of said officer, thoroughly shake the tickets previously deposited in a box, or other safe place of deposit, and draw therefrom promiscuously twenty-four tickets, and the persons whose names are on those twenty-four tickets shall be summoned to serve as a grand jury, a minute of which drawing shall be kept by said Clerk, with the names entered thereon in the order they are drawn; when, if petit jurors are also required, said Clerk shall proceed in like manner to draw and minute twenty-four tickets, and the twenty-four persons named on said tickets shall be summoned to serve as petit jurors; said Clerk and attending officer shall then sign the minutes of the drawing, which minutes shall be filed by said Clerk in the office of the County Court of the county in which said drawing was had.

Marshal proceed to County Court Clerk.

Tickets drawn by lot.

Sec. 7. Upon the conclusion of the drawing, and previous to the filing as aforesaid, said Clerk shall forthwith make a list of the names of the persons drawn, if any, to serve as grand jurors and a list of the names of the persons drawn, if any, to serve as petit jurors, and certify to said list or lists, and deliver it, or them, to the officer having the writ from the Clerk of a District Court to summon jurors.

Make list of Names drawn.

Certify to Lists.

Sec. 8. The officer having the writ and jury list, or lists, in charge as hereinbefore provided shall immedi-

How officer shall summon.

ately upon his reception of said list or lists, proceed to summon the persons named on said list, or lists, to attend said court, specifying the time and place of its sitting; which summons shall be served by giving each person a written notice, or by leaving a copy of the summons at his residence in care of some person of suitable age and discretion.

SEC. 9. If, in summoning the persons named on said list, or lists, said officer becomes aware that, from any cause beyond his control, there will be a failure by one or more of said persons to appear as required, he shall forthwith repair to the aforesaid Clerk of the County Court, who shall with said officer proceed to draw, as hereinbefore provided, until the required number of jurors can be procured: and said officer shall return said list, or lists, and writ to said District Court at the time specified, and shall specify the persons summoned and the manner in which each was summoned. *If not enough names.* *Repair to Clerk of County Court.*

SEC. 10. When a District Court is to be held for a district, and the Judge thereof is reliably advised that the ends of justice will be materially promoted by so doing, said Judge may apportion the twenty-four grand jurors among two or more counties in his district. *District Court for District.* *Judge may apportion.*

SEC. 11. After a grand jury is empanelled, sworn or affirmed and charged by the court, said court shall appoint one of their number to be their foreman, and said foreman shall have power to swear or affirm all witnesses, to testify before said grand jury and shall, when the grand jury or any twelve of them have, upon, to them, good and sufficient evidence, found a bill of indictment, endorse thereon the words, to wit—"A True Bill," and officially sign his name to said endorsement, and also note or cause to be noted on the bill of indictment the name or names of the witnesses upon whose evidence it was found. *12 Grand Jury may indict.*

SEC. 12. The Clerk of the District Court shall write upon separate tickets the names of the persons returned to serve as petit jurors, shall so fold said tickets that their names thereon do not appear, shall deposit them in a box or other safe place of deposit and, when ordered by the Court, draw from said box or place, twelve names: and the persons whose names are drawn shall constitute a petit jury, except such as are legally rejected, and in case of such rejection, said Clerk shall continue to draw until said petit jury is complete, and if the number of the petit jurors returned to said Court *Petty Jurors how chosen.*

Talismen.
shall be exhausted, then the proper officer shall, upon the order of the Judge, summon talismen from the body of the county to complete said panel.

SEC. 13. If, during any term of a District Court, the number of jurors provided proves insufficient, the Clerk of said Court shall immediately issue a writ, directed to one of the officers before named as the persons to serve such writs, for the requisite number; and said officer shall at once proceed to procure them in the manner hereinbefore provided; and in case said writ exhausts the names already selected, the Clerk of the County Court of the proper county shall forthwith call a meeting of said Court, which shall immediately select, in the manner already specified, at least as many names as may at that time be deemed sufficient.

If insufficiency of Jurors how to proceed.

SEC. 14. A District Court is hereby empowered to sit at the county seat of any county, within its district, to try cases arising in such county, whenever three-fourths of the electors in said county shall, in a writing to that effect, signed by them, petition the Judge of the district to hold a term of court in said county: Provided, that the County Court of said county shall make provision to defray the expenses of said District Court.

District Court may sit by petition.

SEC. 15. If any person fails to appear as a grand or petit juror, when lawfully summoned, or if a Marshal or his deputy or any clerk of the district or County Court, or any Sheriff or his deputy, fails to fulfil the duties enjoined upon him in this act, without having a reasonable excuse, he shall be considered guilty of contempt, and may be fined for each offence, for the use of the county in which the defendant resides, in any sum not exceeding fifty dollars; unless, at or before the next term of said District Court, good cause be shown for such failure: Provided, that the oath or affirmation of any such delinquent shall at all times be received as competent evidence in his favor.

If person fails to appear as a Juror.

Fine not exceed $50.

SEC. 16. It shall be the duty of the Clerk of a District Court, at the close of each term of said Court, to make out and give to each juror a certificate, certifying the number of days attendance of, and amount of compensation due to said juror, which certificate, upon being presented to the County Court of the county from which said juror was summoned, shall entitle said juror to be allowed and paid by said county, the sum specified in said certificate, as other demands against the county are paid: Provided, that no juror shall be paid

Juror receive certificate.

Paid by County.

out of the county treasury for any jury service for
which he may have received or be entitled to receive
pay for sitting as a juror upon United States business.

Except on U. S. business.

Sec. 17.   All laws and parts of laws conflicting with
this act are hereby repealed.

Approved Jan. 21, 1859.

Chap. IV.—*An Act prescribing the manner of challenging Petit Jurors.*

Jan. 21, 1859.

Sec. 1.   *Be it enacted by the Governor and Legislative
Assembly of the Territory of Utah,* that, previous to
swearing persons drawn or selected to serve as a petit
jury, each party may challenge said persons for cause,
to the number that either or both parties may be able
to produce, what to them, seems to be good cause, the
validity of said cause to be determined by the court;
and in civil cases, each party may, as aforesaid, pe-
remptorily challenge as many as four of said persons,
and in criminal cases as many as six.

Each party may challenge.

Court deter- mine validity.

Civil cases 4; criminal cases 6.

Sec. 2.   And be it further enacted, that Sec. 12 of
"An Act regulating the mode of procedure in civil
cases in the courts of the Territory of Utah," approved
Dec. 30, 1852, and Sec. 10 of "An Act regulating the
mode of procedure in criminal cases," approved January 21, 1853, are hereby repealed.

Repealing clause.

Approved Jan. 21, 1859.

Chap. V.—*An Act defining the three Judicial Districts for the Districts in the Territory of Utah.*

Jan. 21, 1859.

Sec. 1.   *Be it enacted by the Governor and Legislative
Assembly of the Territory of Utah,* that the First Judicial District shall be composed of Washington, Iron,
Beaver, Millard, San Pete, Juab, Utah and Cedar counties; the Second of Carson, Humboldt and St. Mary
counties; and the Third, of Shambip, Tooele, Great
Salt Lake, Summit, Green River, Davis, Weber, Box
Elder, Cache, Malad, Greasewood and Desert counties:
—and that the "Resolution defining the Judicial Districts for the United States Courts for the Territory of
Utah," approved January 17, 1856, is hereby repealed.

1st District.

2nd   "

3rd   "

Repealing clause.

From 1st May, 1859.

SEC. 2. This act to take effect and be in force from and after the first day of May, A.D. 1859.

APPROVED Jan. 21, 1859.

Jan. 21, 1859.

CHAP. VI.—*An Act assigning the Chief Justice and the two Associate Justices to their several Judicial Districts.*

Be it enacted by the Governor and Legislative Assembly of Chief Justice, *the Territory of Utah,* that the Chief Justice is assigned 1st District. J. Cradlebaugh, to the First Judicial District; the Hon. John Cradle- 2nd District. baugh, Associate Justice, to the Second; and the Hon. C. E. Sinclair, Charles E. Sinclair, Associate Justice, to the Third: and 3rd District. that the Resolution assigning the United States Judges Repealing for Utah to the several Judicial Districts, approved Jan. clause. 17, 1856, is hereby repealed.

APPROVED Jan. 21, 1859.

Jan. 21, 1859.

CHAP. VII.—*An Act establishing the Salaries of certain Terri- torial Officers.*

Be it enacted by the Governor and Legislative Assembly of the Territory of Utah, that there shall be paid, annu- ally, out of any money in the Territorial Treasury not otherwise appropriated, the following sums, to the re- Salaries of Ad- spective officers, herein named, as follows—to wit:— jutant General, Territorial Trea- surer, and Au- ditor.

To the Adjutant General	$300,00
Territorial Treasurer	200,00
Auditor of Public Accounts	200,00

APPROVED Jan. 21, 1859.

Jan. 21, 1859.

CHAP. VIII.—*An Act concerning Notaries Public for Great Salt Lake County.*

Be it enacted by the Governor and Legislative Assembly of the Territory of Utah, that there shall be elected, by the joint vote of this Legislative Assembly, one Notary Public for Great Salt Lake County, in addition to the Two Notaries Notary Public already provided for said county; and for G. S. L. that annually hereafter there shall, in like manner, be County. two Notaries Public elected for Great Salt Lake County.

APPROVED Jan. 21, 1859.

Chap. IX.—*An Act concerning Costs and Fees of Courts, and for* Jan. 21, 1859. *other purposes.*

Sec. 1. *Be it enacted by the Governor and Legislative Assembly of the Territory of Utah,* that the fees and compensation in District Courts, of officers and other persons herein named, shall be as follows:—

Fees District Courts.

The clerk's fees shall be, for issuing and sealing a writ	50c.
Docketing a case 15c. Each subsequent docketing	10c.
Entering judgment on a suit, without process	25c.
Entering cause on judgment docket	20c.
Entering each order of court	20c.
Filing each case in a suit, except appeals	10c.
Entering special bail	20c.
Swearing and empannelling each jury	20c.
Administering oath to each witness on trial	5c.
Entering verdict of jury and judgment	25c.
Entering satisfaction of judgment	5c.
Issuing writ of execution	25c.
Taxing cost	15c.
Entering exonerator	10c.
Entering surrender	10c.
A commission to take depositions	50c.
All motions in one suit	15c.
All the rules in one suit	20c.
If there be but one	10c.
A venire for a jury	25c.
Making a complete record in each cause when ordered by the court for every hundred words	15c.
Copy of record when required per 100 words	10c.
Every certificate when required with seal of court	25c.
A subpena to include all the witnesses called for at the time of issuing	25c.
Filing record of appeal, writ of error, supercedeas, certiorari or habeas corpus	5c.
Recording assessment of damages	15c.
Copy of paper not herein provided, for every hundred words	10c.
For administering oath in naturalization cases	10c.
Filing the same	10c.
For certificate of application	30c.
Certificate of naturalization	50c.
Taking a recognisance	15c.

Each bond required by law   -   -   50c.

Certificate of admission to the bar   -   -   50c.

No fees shall be demanded from grand or petit juries, or witnesses, for issuing a certificate entitling them to fees as such.

County Court
may allow fees
to District Court
Clerk.
Fees of Probate
Clerk same as
District Court
Clerk. A County Court may allow the clerk of a District Court any sum not exceeding $50 per annum for services in criminal cases where the defendants are acquitted; and in all civil and criminal cases, the fees of a clerk of a Probate Court shall be the same as hereinbefore provided for a clerk of a District Court.

Sec. 2.   And be it further enacted, that the fees of the clerk of the Supreme Court shall be, for issuing and sealing each writ   -   75c.

Docketing cause each time   -   -   15c.

Entering cause on judgment docket   -   25c.

Entering each order, motion or rule   -   20c.

Filing each paper   -   -   -   10c.

Entering judgment   -   -   -   35c.

Entering nonsuit, discontinuance, dismissal, or nolle prosequi   -   -   -   15c.

Entering satisfaction of judgment   -   15c.

Entering return of execution   -   -   15c.

Taxing costs   -   -   -   -   25c.

Copy of paper or record per 100 words   -   10c.

Certificate   -   -   -   -   40c.

Taking bond   -   -   -   -   50c.

Assessment of damage   -   -   -   25c.

Entering cause on court calender   -   15c.

Entering appearance of parties   -   -   10c.

Signing final record   -   -   -   20c.

Making complete record per 100 words   -   15c.

Certificate of admission to the bar   - $2,00c.

For all services not specified he shall receive such compensation as shall be allowed a Clerk of a District Court for like services.

Sec. 3.   And be it further enacted, that the fees of the Territorial Marshal or a Sheriff or either of their deputies shall be, for serving any writ and returning the same (subpenas excepted) for one defendant   -   50c.

For each additional defendant   -   -   25c.

Commitment to prison   -   -   -   25c.

Discharge from prison   -   -   -   25c.

Attending with a person before a judge or court,
  when required at any time, not a regular term $1,50c.
Mileage in going with such person before said
  judge and returning, per mile   -   -   5c.
Serving a writ of possession or restitution   -   50c.
Copy of a paper required by law, for each 100
  words   -   -   -   -   15c.
Serving and returning a subpena, for each per-
  son therein named   -   -   -   20c.
Calling a jury in each cause   -   -   20c.
Summoning a grand and petit jury   - $5,00c.
Traveling fees going and returning per mile   5c.
Selling land or other property on execution, per
  day   -   -   -   - $1,50c.
Making and executing a deed for property sold
  on execution   -   -   - $1,00
Serving one person with an order of court, be-
  sides mileage   -   -   -   15c.
Summoning a jury in cases of forcible entry and
  detainer   -   -   - $1,00c.
Serving an execution or order for partition of
  real estate or assigning dower, besides mileage   50c.
Each bond   -   -   -   25c.
For collecting and paying over all sums under
  $200   -   -   -   5 per cent.
All sums over $200 and less than $500   3 per cent.
All sums over $500 and under $1000   2 per cent.
And all over $1000   -   -   1 per cent.
Returning a writ not served   -   -   10c.
Receiving a prisoner on surrender by bail   25c.
Taking new bail   -   -   -   25c.
Dieting a prisoner (to be paid out of the County
  Treasury when the prisoner is insolvent) per
  day   -   -   -   -   35c.
The Territorial Marshal or a Sheriff may be al- | Proper County Court allow $50 to Marshal or Sheriff:
  lowed by the proper County Court, a sum not
  exceeding $50 for services rendered the coun-
  ty, in delivering notices and other duties actually performed for which no specified sum
  is provided by law.
  Sec. 4. Be it further enacted, that the fees of | Fees of County Court Clerks.
    the Clerks of County Courts shall be, for
    recording proceedings in term time, per
    day   -   -   - $2,00c.
For entering other records and accounts kept in
  his office, for each folio of 100 words   -   10c.

For making calculation and carrying out the amount of taxes on the assessment roll, per day	2,00
For making out abstracts of assessment roll, for each 100 words (4 figures counting one word)	10c.
For each bond for an officer, to be paid by such officer	50c.
Filing all returns of an election	50c.
For each certificate	25c.
Copy of any paper or record, per 100 words	10c.
For each advertisement of an election	15c.

Fees of Justice of Peace in civil cases.

Sec. 5. Be it further enacted, that the fees of Justices of the Peace in civil cases shall be,

for docketing each suit	10c.
For summons or warrant	25c.
Precept for jury	15c.
Every subpena including all witnesses asked for at the time	20c.
Swearing a jury	15c.
Entering a verdict	15c.
Entering judgment	25c.
Taking and certifying any acknowledgment	25c.
Administering oath	5c.
Every rule of reference	10c.
Every continuance or adjournment	15c.
Taking depositions, per 100 words	15c.
Certifying a deposition	20c.
Taking bail, recognizances or security	25c.
For every discontinuance or satisfaction	15c.
Entering amicable judgment	25c.
Transfer of judgment	25c.
Filing each paper	5c.
Opening judgment, after default	15c.
Taxing cost	10c.
Issuing writ of attachment	25c.
Taking bond for the same	25c.
For holding inquiry in cases of forcible entry and detainer, in addition to other fees, per day	1,00c.
Writ of restitution, including execution for costs	25c.
Rule to take deposition, when the witness is out of the Territory	25c.
For every execution	25c.
Transcript of judgment, per 100 words	15c.
For hearing any matter wherein a jury is called	25c.
For administering an oath out of court	15c.

When justices are called from their offices, mile-
age per mile   -   -   -   5c.
Copy of the proceedings in any case   -   10c.
Certificate thereof   -   -   -   15c.
Affidavit for attachment   -   -   15c.
For renewing execution   -   -   10c.

SEC. 6. And be it further enacted, that the fees of Justices of the Peace in criminal cases shall be, for warrant or search warrant   -   -   -   -   25c. *Fees of Justice of Peace in criminal cases.*

Commitment to jail   -   -   -   15c.
For affidavit   -   -   -   15c.
Taking recognizance   -   -   25c.
Entering judgment for fine or punishment 25c.
Order of discharge to jailor   -   -   25c.
For other services, fees as in civil cases.

SEC. 7. And be it further enacted, that the fees of a Justice of the Peace, when acting as Coroner to be paid by the estate of the deceased, when solvent, shall be, for summoning and swearing a jury   -   50c. *When acting as coroner.*
For issuing subpena or warrant   -   25c.
For viewing each body, taking and returning inquest to Probate Court   -   -   5,00c.
For other services and expenses, an allowance may be made by the County Courts, not exceeding   -   -   -   12,00c.

SEC. 8. And be it further enacted, that fees of Constables in civil and criminal cases shall be, for serving summons, for each person therein named   -   -   25c. *Fees of Constables.*
For serving warrant   -   -   25c.
Copy of every summons or warrant   -   15c.
Traveling to and from place of service, per mile 5c.
Summoning a jury   -   -   50c.
Attending the same on trial   -   -   50c.
For serving execution   -   -   25c.
Advertising and selling property   -   75c.
Advertising without selling   -   -   25c.
For notifying plaintiff of service   -   20c.
Return of execution, when no levy is made 10c.
Each notice of attachment being issued 15c.
Bond for the same   -   -   25c.
For serving attachment   -   -   50c.
On all sums collected and paid over on executions   -   -   7 per cent.

Serving subpena - - -	15c.
Commitment to prison - -	25c.

Witness fees.

SEC. 9. And be it further enacted, that Witnesses' fees shall be, each witness for a day's attendance before a District or Probate Court   -   -   -   50c.

Attendance before a justice of the peace per day   50c.

Mileage per mile   -   -   -   5c.

To receive pay in advance.

Provided that no witness shall be compelled to attend any Court in civil cases, unless he shall receive, in advance, from the party subpenaing him, his mileage going and returning, and his fee for one day's attendance, and shall not be required to remain in court longer than one day, unless he is paid in advance for each day's attendance.

SEC. 10. Be it further enacted, that Jurors' fees shall be, for grand jurors per day, to

Fees of Grand Jurors, Petit Jurors, and mileage.

be paid by the proper county -	75c.
Petit jurors per day - -	75c.
Mileage per mile - - -	5c.
Jurors each day before a justice of the peace	50c.

Fees of Judges of Probate.

SEC. 11. And be it further enacted, that fees of Judges of Probate shall be, for granting

letters of administrators or probate of wills	1,00c.
When the same are contested - -	1,00c.
Hearing a complaint against spendthrift or lunatic	1,00c.
Appointing a guardian for minor or lunatic	50c.
Decree for probate of will - -	75c.
When contested - - -	1,00c.
Decree for settlement of estate -	50c.
Order for distribution - -	50c.
Examining and allowing inventory, for the first page - - - -	25c.
Every succeeding page - -	10c.
Any writ or process issued under seal -	25c.
Examining and allowing accounts, not exceeding one page - - -	25c.
Every additional page - -	10c.
Warrant to appraise or divide estate -	25c.
Issuing commission to receive and examine claims of creditors when an estate is represented insolvent - - -	25c.
Allowing an appeal - -	25c.
Approving securities of executor or administrator	25c.
Assigning personal estate to widow -	25c.

Assignment of dower in real estate -	25c.
Disallowance of application for letters of adminis- tration, or probate of will, to be paid by the losing party - -	75c.
For every continuance - -	15c.
Order for sale of personal estate -	25c.
Certificate of necessity for sale of real estate	25c.
Extending letters of administration -	50c.
For bonds upon letters of administration or ap- pointment of guardian - -	50c.
Probate of will and letters testamentary thereon	50c.
Drawing a decree respecting the probate of will or codicil - - -	50c.
Bond for the execution - -	25c.
Drawing order of distribution -	25c.
A quietus - - -	25c.
Filing each paper - -	5c.
Administering an oath - -	5c.
Recording all papers required by law to be re- corded, for every one hundred words -	15c.
Appeal or other bonds - -	25c.
A warrant to divide an intestate estate among the heirs, a warrant to set off the widow's dower, or a warrant to receive and examine the claims of an insolvent estate -	25c.
A citation or summons for the first person named therein - - -	25c.
Each other person named therein -	10c.
Entering and filing a caveat - -	15c.
To apportion an insolvent estate among the cred- itors - - -	75c.
Seal to an exemplification - -	15c.
When a translation of any will, deed, or other writing is required he shall be entitled to re- ceive for every one hundred words -	25c.
When sitting on civil or criminal cases per day	$3,00
Hearing each divorce case - -	5,00

SEC. 12. Be it further enacted, that the fees of Notaries Public shall be, for every pro- test with seal - - 1,00

Fees of Nota- ries.

Attesting letters of attorney and seal -	50c.
Drawing and taking proof and acknowledgment of any legal instrument not exceeding two pages - - -	1,00
Certifying power of attorney - -	25c.
Affidavit with seal - -	25c.

Registering protest of bill of exchange   :   50c.

For non-acceptance or non-payment   :   50c.

Drawing and certifying affidavit   :   :   25c.

Each oath or affirmation   :   :   10c.

Every certificate   :   :   :   25c.

Being present at demand, tender or deposit   50c.

Other fees the same as are allowed other officers
in similar cases.

SEC. 13.   In all cases of criminal prosecution, where the complainant is not an eye witness of the crime *When complainant pays costs.* alleged, and the defendant is not found guilty on trial, the complainant shall pay the costs unless probable cause shall have been shown in said trial; and all persons *Persons found guilty pay costs.* found guilty of crime, upon trial, shall pay the costs, except where the party is insolvent, in which case a *County Court authorize payment.* county court may authorize the payment of said costs or such part thereof as their discretion shall dictate, out of the county treasury: Provided, that a county *Not more than one-third county revenue.* court shall not appropriate more than one-third of the county revenue to defray the expenses of courts for any one year; and that in all appropriations of a county court for court expenses, that of dieting prisoners shall have the precedence.

SEC. 14.   The Territorial Marshal or a Sheriff, or *Marshal and sheriffs' fee before Supreme Court.* either of their deputies, shall be allowed one dollar and fifty cents a-day, for every day he shall attend upon the Supreme Court, which compensation may be paid from the territorial treasury.

SEC. 15.   A Sheriff shall be allowed one dollar for every day he is required to attend, and does so attend, *Before District Court.* a district court, which may be paid out of the county treasury of the proper county: Provided, that if a district court shall deem it expedient, said court may make an order to command any number of constables to attend said court, not exceeding three, to be entitled to *Three Constables $1 per day.* one dollar per day each, for every day such constables shall actually attend; and said order shall be entered on the record.

SEC. 16.   Fees of Prosecuting Attorneys in *Prosecuting Attorneys.* the district and probate courts shall be, for drawing an indictment   :   :   75c.

For attendance on the grand jury, for each indictment   :   :   :   :   50c.

For prosecuting each criminal   :   :   3,00c.

For entering nolle prosequi   :   1,00c.

For replying to motion to quash   :   25c.

Replying to demurrer   :   :   25c.
Attendance on district court per day   :   1,00c.
Attendance on probate court per day   :   75c.

That in all cases where fees shall not be collected from complainant or defendant, the county court is authorized to pay, not exceeding fifty per cent of the above costs of attorneys, from the county treasury—and the attorney general may also receive from the territorial treasurer, a sum not exceeding $50 annually, for services rendered in suits to which the Territory is a party. *When County Court to pay.*

SEC. 17. When two or more persons are served, mileage shall be computed by the officer only from the most remote place, unless the places are in opposite directions, and a successful party in any suit shall, in no case, recover the costs of more than two witnesses to one fact. *Mileage how computed.*

SEC. 18. If any officer shall wilfully or corruptly take greater fees than are herein before expressed and limited, for any service to be done by him in his office, or if any person shall charge or demand and take any of the fees hereinbefore ascertained, when the business for which such fees are chargeable shall not have been actually done and performed, such officer, for every such offence, shall, on conviction thereof before any justice of the peace of the proper county, forfeit and pay into the county treasury a sum not exceeding ninety dollars. *Penalty for greater fees.*

Approved Jan 21, 1859.

CHAP. X.—*An Act changing the County Seat of Washington county.*   *Jan. 11, 1859.*

Be it enacted by the Governor and Legislative Assembly of the Territory of Utah, that the County Seat of Washington county is hereby changed from the town of Harmony to the town of Washington, in said county. *Town of Washington.*

Approved Jan. 11, 1859.

CHAP. XI.—*An Act reorganizing Carson and Green River counties, and attaching St. Mary and Humboldt counties.*   *Jan. 17, 1859.*

SEC. 1. *Be it enacted by the Governor and Legislative Assembly of the Territory of Utah*, that the acts attaching Carson and Green River counties to Great Salt Lake

Act repealed. county are hereby repealed, and the former organiza-

Organization revived. tions of said counties revived; and that the records, papers, books, blanks and seals of the Probate and County

Records &c. to probate judges. Courts of said counties, shall be delivered to the respective Probate Judges of said counties.

SEC. 2.   And be it further enacted, that St. Mary and

St. Mary and Humboldt attached. Humboldt counties are hereby attached to Carson coun-

Genoa, county seat of Carson. ty, for election, revenue and judicial purposes: and that
Genoa is hereby made the county seat of Carson county;
and Fort Bridger, that of Green River county.

SEC. 3.   All laws and parts of laws conflicting with
this act are hereby repealed.

Approved Jan. 17, 1859.

Jan. 21, 1859. CHAP. XII.—*An Act apportioning to certain counties, Representatives to the Legislative Assembly.*

SEC. 1.   *Be it enacted by the Governor and Legislative Assembly of the Territory of Utah,* that at the general
election on the first Monday of August 1859, and an-

G. S. L. County 9, Weber 2, Green River 1, Carson 1, Millard 1, Beaver 1. nually thereafter at said general election, Great Salt
Lake county is authorized to elect nine Representatives;
Weber county, two; Green River county, one; Carson
county, one; Millard county, one; and Beaver county,
one.

SEC. 2.   All laws and parts of laws conflicting with
this act are hereby repealed.

Approved Jan. 21, 1859.

Jan. 17, 1859. CHAP. XIII.—*An Act authorizing a Special Election in Lehi City, Utah county.*

SEC. 1.   *Be it enacted by the Governor and Legislative Assembly of the Territory of Utah,* that a special election
shall be held in the city of Lehi on the first Monday of

First Monday in Feb. February next, for the purpose of electing a Mayor,
four Aldermen and nine Councilors, who shall hold
their offices until the first Monday of April eighteen
hundred and sixty; or until their successors shall be
elected and qualified.

SEC. 2.   Such election and all subsequent elections

shall be conducted as provided for in section 5 of "An Act to incorporate the city of Lehi," approved February 5, 1852.

Approved Jan. 17, 1859.

Future elections held.

CHAP. XIV.—*An Act changing the Times of holding Elections in certain Cities.*

Jan. 21, 1859.

SEC. 1. *Be it enacted by the Governor and Legislative Assembly of the Territory of Utah,* that the times of holding elections for city officers, in the cities of Ogden, E. T., Alpine, Lehi, Lake, Pleasant Grove, Provo, Springville, Payson, Nephi, Manti, Fillmore, Parowan and Cedar, are hereby changed to the second Monday in February next; and all subsequent elections shall be held every two years thereafter.

Election second Monday in Feb.

SEC. 2. All laws and parts of laws conflicting with this act are hereby repealed.

SEC. 3. This act shall be in force from and after its passage.

Law in force from passage.

Approved Jan. 21, 1859.

CHAP. XV.—*An Act to provide for the selection and location of a quantity of Land, equal to two townships, for the establishment of a University.*

Jan. 21, 1859.

SEC. 1. *Be it enacted by the Governor and Legislative Assembly of the Territory of Utah,* that there shall be elected by the qualified electors, at the next general election to be held on the first Monday of August, 1859, and annually thereafter, at each subsequent said general election, a Board of Commissioners, to consist of three men, to select and locate, from time to time, as in their judgment they may deem best, a quantity of land equal to two townships, in accordance with the provisions of the third section of an Act of Congress entitled "An Act to establish the office of Surveyor General of Utah, and to grant land for School and University purposes," approved Feb. 21, 1855.

Election of board of Commission — three men.

Two townships.

SEC. 2. Said Commissioners, after being duly sworn faithfully to discharge their duties, shall proceed as soon as practicable after the land shall have been surveyed, to select and locate such lands in such manner as they shall deem proper, or as the Legislative Assembly may

Duly sworn.

direct; and they shall from time to time, inform the Surveyor General of the precise tract or tracts so selected or located, or, should the Surveyor General's office be closed, they shall in like manner inform the Register of the land office, in the district where said tract or tracts are selected or located by them; and **Report annually.** shall annually report and present a schedule of the sections or tracts of lands selected by them, and approved by the Surveyor General, or by a Register or Registers of public lands, as the case may be, to the Legislative Assembly.

Sec. 3.   Said Commissioners shall receive, out of the **Receive compensation.** Territorial Treasury, out of any money not otherwise appropriated, such compensation as may be allowed by the Legislative Assembly, and shall keep a suitable book, in which they shall enter and record the numbers of the sections, or the part or parts thereof, so located by them; and shall transmit to their successors in office all books and papers appertaining to the location of said lands.

Approved Jan. 21, 1859.

Jan. 21, 1859. CHAP. XVI.—*An Act in relation to the entering of Public Lands.*

Sec. 1.   *Be it enacted by the Governor and Legislative Assembly of the Territory of Utah,* that, so soon as a land office shall be established in this Territory, it shall be the duty of the county courts, respectively, to select **County Courts to select quarter section.** and enter a quarter section of land for county purposes, as contemplated in an act of Congress entitled an "Act granting to the counties or parishes of each State and Territory of the United States, in which the public lands are situated, the right of pre-emption to quarter sections of land for seats of justice within the same." Approved May 26, 1824.

Sec. 2.   And be it further enacted, that on petition of the residents of any unincorporated town to the county court, it shall be the duty of said court to select and enter, at the proper land office, not exceeding one half section of the land so occupied, for the several use and benefit of the rightful claimants thereof, according to their respective interests, as contemplated in an act of Congress entitled "An Act for the relief of citizens of towns upon the public lands of the United States under certain circumstances." Approved May 23, 1844."

Provided, the requisite amount of means or money necessary for the purchase of said lands, and the incidental expenses accruing therefrom, be furnished and delivered to the court by the rightful claimants to said lands.

Provided, requisite money be furnished court.

Sec. 3. The county courts, respectively, acting as trustees under the provisions of this act, are hereby authorized and required, on application of the rightful claimants, to execute transfers of said lands held by them in trust, which transfers shall be valid in law; and are further empowered to adopt such rules and regulations as may be necessary to carry into effect the provisions of this act: Provided such rules and regulations do not conflict with the Constitution and laws of the United States, and the laws of this Territory.

County Courts as trustees to execute transfers

Sec. 4. Be it further enacted, that the provisions of this act, so far as applicable, shall apply to the corporate authorities of incorporated towns and cities.

Shall apply to corporate towns, &c.

Approved Jan. 21, 1859.

Chap. XVII.—*An Act extending the time of a Grant to Abiah Wardsworth and others of the bridge across Weber river.*

Jan. 21, 1859.

Be it enacted by the Governor and Legislative Assembly of the Territory of Utah, that the grant to Abiah Wardsworth, Ira N. Spaulding and Willard G. McMullen to construct a toll bridge across Weber river, approved June 4, 1853, is hereby extended to David B. Bybee, and his associates, as the successors of the above named grantees, for the term of three years or until the first day of January 1862; said Bybee and his associates, being entitled to all the privileges, and holden for the faithful performance of every obligation resting upon the original grantees, as contemplated in the aforesaid act.

Toll bridge across Weber.

Grant extended to David B. Bybee.

For three years.

Approved Jan. 21, 1859.

Chap. XVIII.—*An Act granting unto Isaac Bullock and Lewis Robison the right to erect and control Ferries on Green River.*

Jan. 17, 1859.

Sec. 1. *Be it enacted by the Governor and Legislative Assembly of the Territory of Utah,* that the exclusive

Grant.

Three years.

right and privileges of ferries across Green river, in Green River county, in said Territory, be granted unto Isaac Bullock and Lewis Robison for three years from and after the 16th day of May, 1859, and they shall be allowed to take toll at the following rates, viz.:—

For any vehicle together with its loading weighing not over 1000lbs. - - - $1,75

Rates of toll.

For any vehicle together with its loading weighing over 1000 and not over 2000lbs - 2,50

And the rate to increase for each additional 1000lbs - - - 1,00

For each horse, mule, ox, or cow - 50

For each sheep, goat, or swine - - 25

When not required to run.

One third more allowed.

Furnish safe conveyance.

Liable for damage.

Sec. 2. In case of high water, winds, rain or storm of any kind, which render the crossing unsafe, then said ferries shall not be required to run, but any agreement of parties shall be allowed, as to risk and price of crossing: Provided, that nothing herein shall justify the parties in taking more than one third over the within specified rates of toll, but at all suitable times, when the river is not fordable, the said ferries shall be provided with good and sufficient boats for crossing, and the said Isaac Bullock and Lewis Robison should furnish speedy and safe conveyance across said river, and be liable for all damages that shall be sustained through their neglect or carelessness.

Give bond and security.

To indemnify losses.

Bond approved by

Sec. 3. The said Isaac Bullock and Lewis Robison shall on or before the 16th day of May, 1859, give bond and security in the sum of two thousand dollars, payable to the people of the Territory of Utah, for the faithful performance of their duties, as herein required, and to indemnify all persons interested in any loss they may sustain in consequence of neglect or carelessness on their part: said bond to be approved by the Territorial Treasurer and filed in his office.

Sec. 4. All laws and parts of laws conflicting with this act are hereby repealed.

Approved Jan. 17, 1859.

Jan. 11, 1859. CHAP. XIX.—*An Act granting unto Joseph Young the right to establish and control Ferries on Bear river, also a Bridge on the Malad.*

Grant for five years.

Sec. 1. *Be it enacted by the Governor and Legislative Assembly of the Territory of Utah*, that Joseph Young have the right to establish and control a ferry or ferries on Bear river, for the term of five years, from and after January 4, 1859, at such place or places as will best subserve the public interests, between the mouth of said river and the kanyon where the river comes through the mountains.

Sec. 2. The said Joseph Young shall be allowed to take toll at the following rates, viz.:

For any vehicle not over 2000lbs weight	$2,00
For any vehicle over 2000 and less than 3000lbs	4,00
For any vehicle over 3000 and less than 4000lbs	5,00
For all vehicles over 4000lbs	6,00
For all animals with packs, each	1,00
For all horses, mules, jacks, oxen and cows, each	25
For all colts, calves, sheep and hogs, each	10

Rates of toll.

Sec. 3. The said Joseph Young is hereby required to keep a good substantial bridge across the Malad river, on the main road leading to the northern part of this Territory, at a convenient point to accommodate the travel crossing the aforesaid ferry or ferries, for five years from and after January 4, 1859, and is empowered to collect toll at the following rates, viz.:— *To keep substantial bridge.*

For carriages, wagons and carts, each	$1,30
For pack animals, each	20
For all loose horses, mules, jacks, oxen and cows, each	10
For all sheep, colts, calves, goats and hogs, each	2

Rates of toll.

All persons shall pass toll free.

Sec. 4. The said Joseph Young shall give bond and security, to be approved by the Territorial Treasurer, and filed in his office, in the penal sum of one thousand dollars, payable to the people of the Territory of Utah, conditioned for the faithfully carrying into effect the provisions of this act; and to indemnify any person for damages they may sustain on account of the insufficiency of the ferries or bridge, while charging toll thereon. *Give bond, approved by and filed with territorial treasurer.* *Liable for damage.*

Sec. 5. If any person, or persons, shall establish a ferry within the before described limits, on Bear river, or a ferry or bridge on the Malad, and take toll thereon, without a grant from the Legislative Assembly, shall forfeit and pay to the people of the Territory of Utah the sum of five hundred dollars for each offence, to be collected as in an action of debt. *If any other establish ferry, &c., forfeit $500. How collected.*

Sec. 6. All acts or parts of acts in any wise conflicting with this act are hereby repealed.

Approved Jan 11, 1859.

4

Jan. 21, 1859. CHAP. XX.—*An Act to incorporate the Placerville, Humboldt and Salt Lake Telegraph Company.*

SEC. 1. *Be it enacted by the Governor and Legislative Assembly of the Territory of Utah,* that Frederick A. Bee, Peter Loveall, Edgar Bogardus, Hosea Stout and Jesse C. Little, their associates and successors, be and they are hereby created a body corporate and politic, to be known by the name and style of "Placerville, Humboldt and Salt Lake Telegraph Company," for the purpose of constructing, extending, and putting in good working order, and of keeping the same in such order and operation, a line or lines of electro magnetic telegraph wires; including the usual insulators, fixtures, materials, stations, electric fluids and other things necessary and proper to conduct and keep the same telegraph line in successful operation, for the transmission of telegrams in the usual way, by such line or lines of wires as aforesaid.

Fred. A. Bee, E. Bogardus, H. Stout, J. C. Little. Body corporate.

Electro Magnetic Telegraph.

To keep in operation.

SEC. 2. Said company shall have power in their corporate name to sue and be sued, to defend and be defended in all courts of law and equity; to hold, lease, or convey property, real or personal, and shall have perpetual succession for the term of fifty years, and may have a corporate seal which they may use and alter at pleasure.

Powers of company.

Fifty years.

SEC. 3. The capital stock of said company shall be fifteen thousand dollars, and may be increased to one hundred and fifty thousand dollars, by a two-third vote of the stockholders of the company: each share to be valued at one hundred dollars, and shall entitle the holder thereof to one vote.

$15,000 an increase to $150,000.

One vote for each share.

SEC. 4. The said telegraph company shall have the power to make such needful regulations and rules as may be necessary to carry into effect the provisions of this act:—Provided, they do not conflict with the laws of the United States or of this Territory.

APPROVED Jan. 21, 1859.

Jan. 11, 1859. CHAP. XXI.—*An Act in relation to Territorial Revenue.*

SEC. 1. *Be it enacted by the Governor and Legislative Assembly of the Territory of Utah,* that for the current year, and annually thereafter, until otherwise directed by legislative enactment, a tax of one fourth of one

Tax one-fourth of a per cent.

per cent. be assessed and collected in accordance with "An Act prescribing the manner of assessing and collecting Territorial and County Taxes," approved January 7, 1854.

Sec. 2. That all acts and parts of acts conflicting with this act are hereby repealed.

Repealing clause.

Approved Jan. 11, 1859.

Chap. XXII.—*An Act amending an Act prescribing the manner of Assessing and Collecting Territorial and County Taxes.*

Jan. 21, 1859.

Sec. 1. *Be it enacted by the Governor and Legislative Assembly of the Territory of Utah,* that the time required by law for the assessment of property, to be made between the first day of January and the first day March, in each year, as provided in the 6th sec. of the act to which this is an amendment, is hereby extended to the first Monday in June in each year.

Time extended to June.

Sec. 2. And all business that relates to the adjudicating the complaints of tax-payers, for erroneous assessments, shall hereafter be done at the June term of the county court, instead of their March term, except in such cases as herein provided for in section four of this act.

Complaints heard at June term of county court.

Sec. 3. The county courts may, at any regular or special term of their court, fix the rate per cent. of taxes for the current year, and shall furnish the assessor and collector, as soon as practicable after his appointment and qualification, with a tax list, as now provided in the 7th section of the aforesaid act, who is hereby authorized to collect, at any time thereafter, the tax due on all property that is intended to be removed from the county previous to the usual time of collection.

County court fix rate; furnish tax list.

Sec. 4. Any person feeling aggrieved at the assessment made by the assessor or his deputy, and being desirous to remove his property from the county, before the proper time for adjudication of such cases, as by law provided, may give notice to the probate judge of said county, who shall immediately cause a special term (if required) of the court to be held, and shall adjudicate all such cases as may be presented.

Person aggrieved to give notice.

Probate court may try the case.

Sec. 5. That hereafter all funds collected by assessors and collectors shall be paid over to the respective territorial or county treasurers in the kind collected.

Funds paid over to treasurers.

SEC. 6. All laws and parts of laws conflicting with this act are hereby repealed.

APPROVED Jan. 21, 1859.

Jan. 21, 1859. CHAP. XXIII.—*An Act appropriating money to the Deseret Agricultural and Manufacturing Society.*

Be it enacted by the Governor and Legislative Assembly of the Territory of Utah, that there be paid out of the territorial treasury, out of any money not otherwise $1000. appropriated, the sum of one thousand dollars, for the benefit of the Deseret Agricultural and Manufacturing Society.

APPROVED Jan. 21, 1859.

Jan. 17, 1859. CHAP. XXIV.—*An Act creating a Special Committee, prescribing their duties, providing for the payment of their services, and their consequent necessary expenses.*

SEC. 1. *Be it enacted by the Governor and Legislative Three men. Assembly of the Territory of Utah*, that a special committee of three men be elected by the joint vote of this Legislative Assembly, whose duty it shall be to prepare, Arrange and arrange and index a code of laws of a general nature, index laws. Report to next applicable to this Territory, and report said code to session. said Assembly during its next session.

SEC. 2. And be it further enacted, that said committee To provide sta- mittee shall have authority and power to provide the tionery, &c. stationery, fuel and rooms requisite to enable them to fulfil the duties herein before specified; the cost of which, $3 per day. and three dollars a day each for the services of said committee, shall be audited and paid out of any money in the territorial treasury, not otherwise appropriated.

SEC. 3. And be it further enacted, that "An Act creating the office of Code Commissioners, and pre- Repealing scribing their duties," approved January 16, 1852, is clause. hereby repealed.

APPROVED Jan. 17, 1859.

Jan. 21, 1859.   CHAP. XXV.—*Territorial Appropriation Bill.*

SEC 1. *Be it enacted by the Governor and Legislative Assembly of the Territory of Utah*, that there be paid out of any money in the territorial treasury, not otherwise appropriated, the following amounts:—

To William C. Staines, as librarian, for binding books, &c. - - - $150.00 W. C. Staines.

To Hosea Stout, for services on Code Commission 1856-7 - - - 174.00 H. Stout.

To James W. Cummings, for services on Code Commission 1856-7 - - - 33.00 J. W. Cummings.

To Samuel W. Richards, for services on Code Commission 1856-7 - - - 105.00 S. W. Richards.

To John T. Caine, as clerk for Code Commission - - - - 249.00 J. T. Caine.

To Wm. H. Hooper, for stationery - 17.75 W. H. Hooper.

To cover the amount drawn by the Warden of the Penitentiary, to defray the expense of territorial prisoners, and the repairs of the Penitentiary up to this date - - 1,245.24 Warden of Penitentiary.

To James Ferguson, for services as Adjutant-General, office rent, stationery, lights, &c. for two years ending Jan. 1, 1859 - 1000.00 J. Ferguson.

To James W. Cummings, for services as Auditor of Public Accounts, for two years to January 1, 1858 - - - 600.00 J. W. Cummings.

To Thomas Bullock, for eight days service as clerk for the committee on compilation of the laws of Utah Territory - - 24.00 T. Bullock.

To Robert L. Campbell, five days - - 15.00 R. L. Campbell.

To John L. Smith, three days - - 9.00 J. L. Smith.

To Leo Hawkins, for twelve days at the close of the session, examining and preparing Laws and Journals for publication - 36.00 L. Hawkins.

To Thomas Bullock, for twelve days, do do 36.00 T. Bullock.

To Edward Hunter, twelve days, rent of office - - - - - - 12.00 E. Hunter.

To Edward Hunter, one load of wood - 8.00

" " 6lbs of candles - 3.00

To H. B. Clawson, for services as Treasurer, two years ending Jan. 1, 1859 - - 400.00 H. B. Clawson.

To Deseret News Office, as per bill rendered 240.25 Deseret News office.

To Hosea Stout, for past services as Attorney General - - - - - 500.00 H. Stout.

To Daniel Carn, for further relief for services of the Penitentiary - - - 1000.00 D. Carn.

To repairing bridge over Provo river near Provo city, or so much thereof as may be necessary - - - - 500.00 Repairing bridge.

| Repairing bridge. | To repairing the bridge over the Sevier river, or so much thereof as may be necessary | 200.00 |

Said repairing to be done under the designated supervision of the county court of the counties in which said bridges are located.

To improve road. To improving the road between Harmony and Washington   250.00

Said improving to be done under the direction and supervision of the county court of Washington county.

T. D. Brown. To Thomas D. Brown, for services rendered as Territorial Road Commissioner, in 1856-57   25.00

$6,832.25. Amount of Territorial Appropriation Bill, six thousand eight hundred and thirty-two dollars and twenty-five cents.

·Approved Jan. 21, 1859.

Jan. 21, 1859.

Chap. XXVI.—*General Appropriation Bill.*

Be it enacted by the Governor and Legislative Assembly of the Territory of Utah, that there be appropriated, out of the monies appropriated by Congress, to defray Legislative expenses in the Territory of Utah, the following amounts to defray the expenses of the present Legislative Assembly, to wit:—

Mileage, council. For mileage of members of the council, five hundred, thirty-eight dollars and fifty cents   538.50

Mileage, house. For mileage of the members of the House of Representatives, one thousand two hundred and six dollars   1,206.00

Per diem, council. For per diem of the members of the Council, one thousand, five hundred and sixty dollars   1,560.00

Per diem, house. For per diem of the members of the House of Representatives, three thousand one hundred and twenty dollars   3,120.00

For per diem of Officers of the Council, eight hundred and forty dollars   840.00

" officers. For per diem of Officers of the House of Representatives, nine hundred and sixty dollars   960.00

Public printing. For public printing, six thousand dollars   6,000.00

Incidentals. For incidental expenses, five thousand dollars   5,000.00

Total, nineteen thousand, two hundred and
  twenty-four dollars and fifty cents   19,224.50
APPROVED Jan. 21, 1859.

CHAP. XXVII.—*Resolution in relation to notifying persons* Jan. 21, 1859.
  elected to office by joint vote of the Assembly.

*Be it resolved by the Governor and Legislative Assembly
of the Territory of Utah,* that it shall be the duty of
the Secretary of the Council, and the Chief Clerk of   Chief clerk to
the House, to issue a certificate to each person elected issue certificate,
by the joint vote of the Legislative Assembly, notifying
them of the office to which they have been elected.
  APPROVED Jan 21, 1859.

CHAP. XXVIII.—*Resolution relating to the Publishing and Dis-* Jan. 21, 1859.
  tribution of the Laws and Journals of the present Session.

*Be it resolved by the Governor and Legislative Assembly
of the Territory of Utah,* that the public printer for this
Legislative Assembly, is hereby authorized and required
to print and publish, in pamphlet form, one thousand   1000 copies of
copies of the Laws and five hundred copies of the Jour-   Laws. 500 copies of
nals of the present session of the Legislative Assembly: Journals.
the Journals to include the Governor's Message and
Proclamations, Auditor's Report, and Territorial Treasurer's Report.
  And be it further resolved, that the Secretary of the   Distribution of
Territory is hereby required to furnish the President of   Laws and Jour-
the United States, and each of his Cabinet, the Presi-   nals.
dent of the Senate, the Speaker of the House of Representatives, and the Governor of each State and Territory of the United States, with one copy each, of the
Laws and Journals, and the Governor of Utah with five
copies of each: one copy of the Laws and Journals to
each member and officer of the present Legislative Assembly: one copy of the Laws to the Judges and Clerks
of the Supreme, District and Probate Courts in this
Territory; to the United States and Territorial Marshal;
to the United States District Attorney and Attorney-
General for the Territory; and to each additional civil
officer in the Territory, including the Mayor, Aldermen,
Recorder and Marshal for each incorporated city; one
copy of the Laws to the Commandant of the Nauvoo
Legion, the Commandants of each Brigade, Regiment

and Battalion and their respective Staff officers—and
two copies of the Laws and Journals to each Public
Library in the Territory.

APPROVED Jan. 21, 1859.

CHAP. XXIX.—*Memorial to Congress for an Act authorizing the
purchase of Indian Lands in Utah, and locating the Indians on
Reserves.*

*To the Honorable, the Senate and House of Representa-
tives of the United States, in Congress assembled:—*

Your memorialists, the Governor and Legislative Assembly of the Territory of Utah, respectfully and earnestly petition your honorably body to pass an act authorizing the Superintendent of Indian Affairs, or the
appointment of a commission whose duty it shall be to
treat with, and purchase the lands belonging to the various tribes of Indians, situated in this Territory, to
wit: The Shoshone or Snake, Pahvante, San Pitch,
Piedes, Cumembahs, or Snake. Diggers, Uinta and
Yampa Utes and other bands; and that it shall be the
duty of the said Superintendent or commission, to locate said Indians on reservations of land, at suitable
distances from white settlers.

Your memorialists do also respectfully petition your
honorable body, to appropriate a sum sufficient to effect
the treaties, purchases, removals, and locations contemplated in this memorial, and also for establishing schools,
erecting mills, furnishing tools for labor and teachers
for the Indians.

Your memorialists respectfully represent, that the
best tract of country, on which to locate the Indians
within our Territory, is situated at the junction of the
Bear and Little Snake rivers, where they may obtain
plenty of fish, a comfortable supply of elk, antelope,
deer and buffalo, while the land is suitable for exten-
sive cultivation, and possesses suitable mill sites. This
location possesses the further advantages of being sufficiently near the white settlements for all purposes of
trade and supervision; and it is sufficiently remote to
prevent sudden outbreaks from the Indians, or illegal
trade by the settlers. In cases of hostility, the country is easily reconnoitred, and is within efficient striking
distance of our garrisons; besides, while to the citizens

it would afford all the benefits of an effectual removal, to the Indians it would possess scarcely the grievance of a removal at all, as in that region great numbers of the Indians have been accustomed to assemble.

The early attention, and favorable consideration of your honorable body, to this very important subject is earnestly and respectfully solicited and your memorialists as in duty bound will ever pray.

APPROVED Jan. 12, 1859.

CHAP. XXX.—*Memorial to Congress for donation of Public Lands to Settlers.* Jan. 11, 1859.

To the Honorable, the Senate and House of Representatives of the United States in Congress assembled:—

Your memorialists, the Governor and Legislative Assembly of the Territory of Utah, respectfully pray your honorable body to extend to this Territory and its inhabitants, the same privileges and donations of land to settlers, as were extended unto the people of Oregon, by the provisions of an act making donations of lands to settlers, approved Sept. 27, 1850, thereby granting to the hardy pioneers of the desert the simple boon of a home, free of charge, as a partial reward for the exposure, difficulties, privations and dangers that have been encountered by the early settlers of this wild and desert Territory. The favorable consideration of your honorable body to this important subject, at an early day, is earnestly and respectfully solicited; and your memorialists as in duty bound will ever pray.

Donate lands to settlers.

APPROVED Jan. 11, 1859.

CHAP. XXXI.—*Memorial to Congress for the Pre-emption of Irrigated Lands.* Jan. 12, 1859.

To the Honorable, the Senate and House of Representatives, in Congress assembled:—

Your memorialists, the Governor and Legislative Assembly of the Territory of Utah, would respectfully represent, that in the settlement of this wild and desert country, it was found necessary to locate in cities, towns, villages, and forts, for mutual protection against the savages; and to enable the settlers to irrigate the lands, they were under the necessity of surveying and enclos-

5

ing small tracts of from one to forty acres each; very few however exceed twenty acres. By this means, in locating almost every settlement, from fifty to one hundred farmers cultivate the same section, which is watered by a canal owned by each agriculturist, in proportion to the area of his farm, meadow or garden; the waters of said canal being distributed to each man in a separate water ditch; a hundred or more of these streams water every section cultivated.

Your memorialists would therefore respectfully pray your honorable body, to pass a law, enabling the occupants of such portions of land, to appoint one of their number an agent, who shall be authorized to pre-empt and enter said lands in a body, and distribute the same by giving titles to the proper claimants. And your petitioners as in duty bound, &c.

APPROVED Jan. 12, 1859.

Jan. 17, 1859. CHAP. XXXII.—*Memorial for an Appropriation, to defray the Expenses of suppressing Indian Hostilities, in the Territory of Utah, in the years eighteen hundred and fifty-three and eighteen hundred and fifty-six.*

To the Honorable, the Senate and House of Representatives of the United States, in Congress assembled:—

We, your memorialists, the Governor and Legislative Assembly of the Territory of Utah, respectfully represent to your honorable body that, in the year eighteen hundred and fifty-three, there was a general Indian war in this Territory, commencing early in the summer and continuing throughout the year, extending through all the settlements east of the Great American Desert; which rendered it necessary to bring to bear upon the various tribes committing these depredations, the entire military force of the Territory.

Early in the year eighteen hundred and fifty-six, Indian hostilities again commenced, known commonly as "Tintick's War," in the counties of Cedar, Utah and Juab, which continued until the ensuing fall.

In suppressing these Indian hostilities, during the year above mentioned, the sum of one hundred and fifty thousand dollars was expended; which sum has been paid by this Territory.

Your memorialists therefore respectfully pray your honorable body, to appropriate the sum of one hundred and fifty thousand dollars, to reimburse the Territory of Utah to the amount thus expended, in protecting the lives and property of her citizens, in their isolated condition, from the numerous lawless and savage bands of Indians who roam in countless numbers through the wild and mountainous country which we inhabit; and as in duty bound, your memorialists will ever pray.

APPROVED Jan. 17, 1859.

CHAP. XXXIII.—*Memorial for the admission of the State of Deseret.*

To the Honorable, the Senate and House of Representatives of the United States in Congress assembled:—

GENTLEMEN:—

Your memorialists, the Legislative Assembly of the Territory of Utah, respectfully represent that in the year 1856, on the 16th day of February, the qualified electors of the Territory of Utah met at the usual places of holding elections in their several precincts, and did unanimously elect, by vote, thirty-nine delegates to a convention, which convention met on the 17th day of March, 1857, in Great Salt Lake City, and appointed a president and secretary, and did proceed to form and adopt a Constitution and a republican form of State government for the Territory of Utah, under the name and style of the "State of Deseret," and prepared a Memorial to your honorable body for admission into the Union, and appointed delegates to transmit the same to Washington city, D.C., which Constitution and Memorial were submitted to the people on the 6th day of April, in their several precincts, and by a unanimous vote approved; and

Whereas, said Constitution has been presented to your honorable body without receiving that favorable action which our constituents desire; and

Whereas, the people of the Territory are abundantly able to support a State government:

Therefore your petitioners respectfully pray your honorable body to admit the State of Deseret into the Union on an equal footing with the original States, thereby to avoid, in a great measure, the difficulties which naturally hinder the advance of the glorious principles of true republicanism, or government by the people, the only sure basis of permanent government the common defence, and to preserve inviolable our national union than to bind the east and west by a magnetic stream, making the inhabitants of our eastern and western limits neighbors by instantaneous communication; and your memorialists, as in duty bound, will ever pray.

CHAP. XXXVIII.—*Memorial to Congress, for the Election of Governor, Judges, Secretary and other Territorial Officers, by the People.*

Your memorialists, the Legislative Assembly of the Territory of Utah, respectfully pray your honorable body to so amend the Organic Act of the Territory of Utah as to extend to the people of this Territory the right of the elective franchise, authorizing them to elect their own Governor, Judges, Secretary, as well as other officers. Your memorialists would respectfully desire your early attention to this subject.

Your memorialists believe that the appointing of strangers, as officers over the citizens of the United States in Territories, (though a time honored custom) is, to say the least, a rule of British colonial rule, and a direct infringement upon the rights of self government, and opposed to the genius and policy of republican institutions. Your attention to this important subject is respectfully requested.

As your honorable body are well aware that no persons can be so well qualified to administer justice, make laws and execute them, in a Territory, as those citizens of the United States who have reclaimed it from a wilderness. The consummation of this valuable reform is respectfully desired; and your memorialists, as in duty bound, will every pray.

CHAP. XXXIX.—*Memorial to Congress in relation to the Unpaid Expenses of the Legislative Assembly of Utah Territory for the Sessions of 1856-7 and 1857-8.*

To the Honorable the Senate and House of Representatives of the United States, in Congress assembled:—

Your memorialists, the Legislative Assembly of the Territory of Utah, would respectfully represent that the expenses of the Legislative Assembly of this Territory for the Sessions of 1856-7 and 1857-8, have not been paid; and that the appropriations justly made by Congress for that purpose have been withheld from their legitimate channel for some cause to your memorialists unknown.

Your memorialists beg leave to respectfully represent, that the sessions of the Legislative Assembly above referred to, were held in strict accordance with the Organic Act and laws of this Territory enacted in strict accordance therewith, and feeling confident of the just and humane intentions of your honorable body in making said appropriations. We respectfully desire, if not inconsistent with your legislative position, that you will take such measures as will cause them to be paid according to the requirements of law. The incalculable inconvenience that has arisen to the people of the Territory by the non-distribution of the laws, and by other difficulties resulting therefrom, are a sufficient reason for presenting this matter before your honorable body. And, as in duty bound, we will ever pray.

Chap. XL.—*Resolutions offered by Hon. O. Hyde.*

Be it resolved by the Legislative Assembly of the Territory of Utah, in joint session, that we highly appreciate the labors and services of His Excellency Governor A. Cumming, in correctly reporting to the government at Washington concerning the public records and library of this Territory; and

Be it further resolved, that his general bearing towards the citizens of Utah has been gentlemanly, courteous and satisfactory; and that his firm, independent, and impartial course has given strength and power to his administration, and his skill and wisdom have essentially aided in preserving the public peace; and that these resolutions be published in the Deseret *News.*

Great Salt Lake City, Jan. 21, 1859.

the common defence, and to preserve inviolable our
national union than to bind the east and west by a magnetic stream, making the inhabitants of our eastern and
western limits neighbors by instantaneous communication; and your memorialists, as in duty bound, will
ever pray.

CHAP. XXXVIII.—*Memorial to Congress, for the Election of
Governor, Judges, Secretary and other Territorial Officers, by
the People.*

Your memorialists, the Legislative Assembly of the
Territory of Utah, respectfully pray your honorable
body to so amend the Organic Act of the Territory of
Utah as to extend to the people of this Territory the
right of the elective franchise, authorizing them to elect
their own Governor, Judges, Secretary, as well as other
officers. Your memorialists would respectfully desire
your early attention to this subject.

Your memorialists believe that the appointing of
strangers, as officers over the citizens of the United
States in Territories, (though a time honored custom)
is, to say the least, a rule of British colonial rule, and a
direct infringement upon the rights of self government,
and opposed to the genius and policy of republican institutions. Your attention to this important subject is
respectfully requested.

As your honorable body are well aware that no persons can be so well qualified to administer justice, make
laws and execute them, in a Territory, as those citizens
of the United States who have reclaimed it from a wilderness. The consummation of this valuable reform is
respectfully desired; and your memorialists, as in duty
bound, will every pray.

CHAP. XXXIX.—*Memorial to Congress in relation to the Unpaid
Expenses of the Legislative Assembly of Utah Territory for the
Sessions of* 1856-7 *and* 1857-8.

*To the Honorable the Senate and House of Representatives
of the United States, in Congress assembled:—*

Your memorialists, the Legislative Assembly of the
Territory of Utah, would respectfully represent that the

expenses of the Legislative Assembly of this Territory for the Sessions of 1856-7 and 1857-8, have not been paid; and that the appropriations justly made by Congress for that purpose have been withheld from their legitimate channel for some cause to your memorialists unknown.

Your memorialists beg leave to respectfully represent, that the sessions of the Legislative Assembly above referred to, were held in strict accordance with the Organic Act and laws of this Territory enacted in strict accordance therewith, and feeling confident of the just and humane intentions of your honorable body in making said appropriations. We respectfully desire, if not inconsistent with your legislative position, that you will take such measures as will cause them to be paid according to the requirements of law. The incalculable inconvenience that has arisen to the people of the Territory by the non-distribution of the laws, and by other difficulties resulting therefrom, are a sufficient reason for presenting this matter before your honorable body. And, as in duty bound, we will ever pray.

CHAP. XL.—*Resolutions offered by Hon. O. Hyde.*

Be it resolved by the Legislative Assembly of the Territory of Utah, in joint session, that we highly appreciate the labors and services of His Excellency Governor A. Cumming, in correctly reporting to the government at Washington concerning the public records and library of this Territory; and

Be it further resolved, that his general bearing towards the citizens of Utah has been gentlemanly, courteous and satisfactory; and that his firm, independent, and impartial course has given strength and power to his administration, and his skill and wisdom have essentially aided in preserving the public peace; and that these resolutions be published in the Deseret *News.*

Great Salt Lake City, Jan. 21, 1859.

INDEX

TO THE

ACTS, RESOLUTIONS AND MEMORIALS

OF THE

LEGISLATIVE ASSEMBLY.

ERRATA.—On the 9th page, chap. 5, in heading, for "Districts in the Territory" read "District Courts in the Territory."